This igloo book belongs to:

....

igloobooks

Published in 2017
by Igloo Books Ltd
Cottage Farm
Sywell
NN6 0BJ
www.igloobooks.com

LEO002 0517
2 4 6 8 10 9 7 5 3 1
ISBN 978-1-78670-461-0

Illustrated by Ralanna Forbis
Written by Jennifer Fujita

Cover designed by Nicholas Gage
Interiors designed by Katie Messenger
Edited by Natalia Boileau

Printed and manufactured in China

My Little Fairy

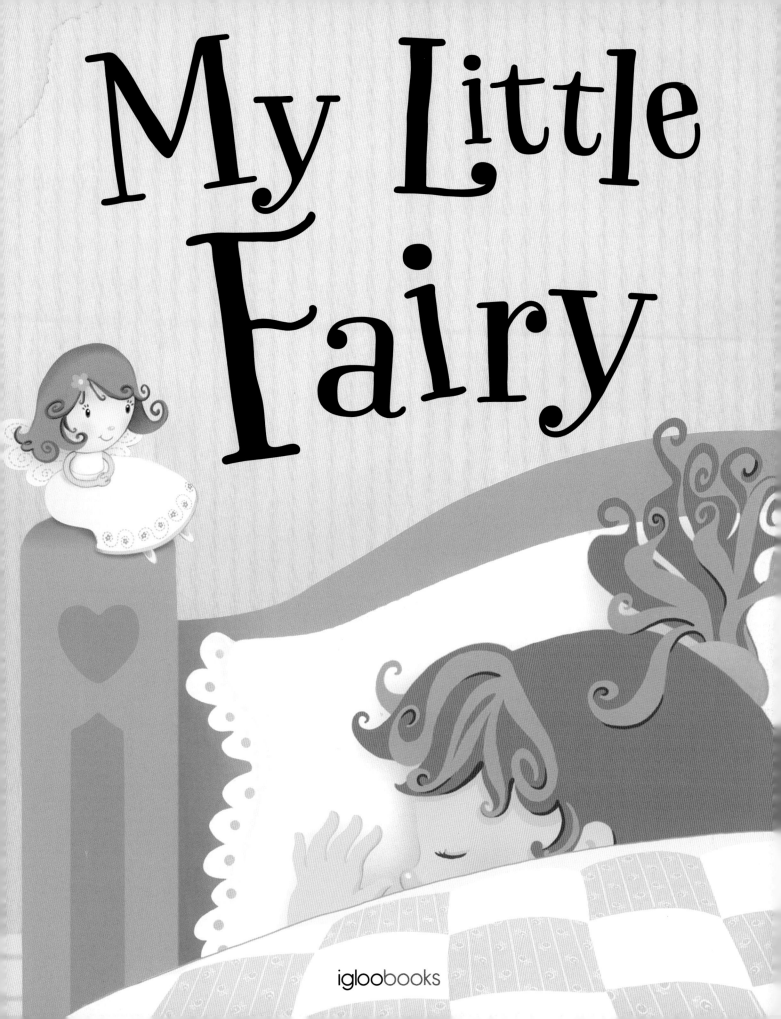

igloobooks

A fairy watches over everything I do.

Every morning, my fairy greets me with a cheery,
"Rise and shine!"

Then we like to wake the others.

"Get out of bed, sleepyheads!" we sing.

When it's time to get dressed, she says,
"We look wonderful!"

My fairy says that a yummy breakfast is the most important meal of the day.

When I play on my bike, my fairy says,
"Let's put our helmets on!"

Wherever I go, whatever I do,
my fairy keeps me safe.

I'm glad my fairy is there
whenever I feel sad...

... or scared...

... or bored indoors on rainy days.

My fairy calms me down.

My fairy cheers me up.

My fairy helps me listen
and do my best...

... because that's what
fairies are for.

My fairy finds the fun in everything.

My fairy keeps my secrets and always makes me laugh.

She's everything a good friend ought to be.

And as I grow...

... I know my fairy will be there for me.

Because she's always watching over me.